The Blue Ghost

by Marion Dane Bauer
illustrated by Suling Wang

A STEPPING STONE BOOK™
Random House New York

For Zoe and her mum, Megan
—M.D.B.

Text copyright © 2005 by Marion Dane Bauer.
Interior illustrations copyright © 2005 by Suling Wang.
Cover illustration copyright © 2005 by Carol Heyer.
All rights reserved under International and Pan-American Copyright Conventions. Published in the United States by Random House Children's Books, a division of Random House, Inc., New York, and simultaneously in Canada by Random House of Canada Limited, Toronto.

www.steppingstonesbooks.com
www.randomhouse.com/kids

Library of Congress Cataloging-in-Publication Data
Bauer, Marion Dane.
The blue ghost / by Marion Dane Bauer ; illustrated by Suling Wang.
    p.   cm.
"A Stepping Stone book."
SUMMARY: At her grandmother's log cabin, nine-year-old Liz is led to make contact with children she believes may be her ancestors.
ISBN 0-375-83179-7 (hardcover) — ISBN 0-375-93179-1 (lib. bdg.) — ISBN 0-375-83339-0 (pbk.)
[1. Guardian angels—Fiction. 2. Ghosts—Fiction. 3. Time travel—Fiction. 4. Grandmothers—Fiction.] I. Wang, Suling, ill. II. Title.
PZ7.B3262Bl 2005   [Fic]—dc22   2004024272

Printed in the United States of America   First Edition   10 9 8 7 6 5 4 3 2 1

RANDOM HOUSE and colophon are registered trademarks and A STEPPING STONE BOOK and colophon are trademarks of Random House, Inc.

Contents

1
The Blue Light

Liz bolted straight up in bed. She stared into the inky darkness. She had no idea what woke her. For a minute she couldn't even remember where she was.

Then she did. She was with her grandmother in the house Gran had grown up in. It was an old house deep in the forests of northern Minnesota. That's why everything was so dark. The only light came from the distant moon.

Liz lay back down. She closed her eyes against the dark.

"Elizabeth." It was just a whisper, but very clear. "Elizabeth!"

Liz jerked upright again as if she were pulled by a string. That was it! That was what woke her up the first time. That voice!

But no one called her *Elizabeth*. Not even Gran. For all her nine years she had been Liz.

"Elizabeth," the voice whispered again.

It wasn't Gran's voice. Liz was certain.

Liz pulled her knees up to her chest. She sat back against the wall. She squeezed her eyes shut and listened hard. She heard nothing more. Only the wind in the trees. Only water lapping lightly against the lakeshore.

She let her eyelids drift open. A blue light hovered near the window on the wall opposite her bed. The light came to rest on the curved lid of the large wooden trunk under the window.

Now it sank down in front of the trunk and circled it. The blue light paused over the top again. Then it floated away. It moved along the wall. When it came to the far corner, the blue light turned and started toward Liz.

Liz opened her mouth to call for her grandmother. Nothing came out but a gasp.

The light moved closer. It grew larger as it approached.

It had a shape now . . . or almost a shape. It seemed to form a person, a woman. One second Liz could see her clearly. She could make out the long, old-fashioned dress. She could see the woman's hair was pulled back in a bun. Then the figure wavered like smoke in a puff of wind.

Liz stared. She wanted to close her eyes. She wanted to cover her face with her hands. But she could only stare.

The woman grew more solid. She
floated right over Liz's head. She was so
close, Liz could have reached out to touch
her . . . if Liz had wanted to touch her.

Now the blue woman looked back at

Liz. "Elizabeth," she whispered again. She sounded sad.

"Yes," Liz replied. Her voice trembled. "Yes?"

The woman didn't speak again. She motioned, as if she wanted Liz to follow. Then she vanished.

Liz lifted a hand to reach for the woman. Her fingers touched the place where the figure had disappeared. There was only wall. Solid wall.

2
Connections

The morning sunshine crept silently into the small bedroom. Liz turned over and squinted at the window on the opposite side of the room.

No wonder the room had been so dark the night before. Even sunlight could barely make its way through the tall pine trees around the house. Not much light passed through the window, either. It was small and deep-set.

What a strange room this was! It was made of logs. The bark had been stripped and the smooth wood polished to a dark gold. Only the wall next to her bed was ordinary. Liz ran a hand over its flatness.

The wall! Liz pulled her hand back as if she had been burned. She sat up.

What had happened last night? Really. Had someone called "Elizabeth"? Had a woman made of blue light appeared on the other side of the room? Over that trunk? And had she called Liz's name again before she disappeared right through this wall?

The idea was silly. Liz was too old to believe in ghosts. Still, she laid a hand on the wall once again where the woman had vanished. She pushed. The wall didn't give. What did she expect? Walls didn't do that.

So it had been a dream, after all. A strange dream. She must have dreamed being awake and sitting up in bed, too. She had never had a dream that seemed so real, though.

Quickly Liz pulled a pair of shorts and a T-shirt from her suitcase. Then she headed for the kitchen. It was empty. Where was her grandmother?

She looked around the kitchen. This room was made of logs, too. Only the wall shared with the small bedroom was an ordinary flat one. She hadn't noticed any of these details last night. She and Gran had arrived late after the long drive from Minneapolis.

Liz stepped outside. She moved out into the yard, then she turned back to look at the house. The oldest parts of the house looked like they had once been a log cabin. Someone had built onto the cabin, both out and up. They had built in a rather helter-skelter fashion, too. The house seemed to stick out in every direction at once.

"It's a hodgepodge, isn't it?"

Liz jumped. It was Gran, speaking Liz's very thoughts. She had stepped out of the forest. In her hands she carried a bouquet of wildflowers. "My great-grandfather built the log cabin," Gran added. She joined Liz in the yard. "Then my grandfather added

onto it. Every time a new child was born, he built another bedroom. So the whole house just grew like Topsy."

"The kitchen and my bedroom used to be the log cabin. Right?" Liz asked.

"Right." Gran studied the house, too. "Back then it was all one room. The wall between your bedroom and the kitchen was added later."

The wall the blue woman had walked through!

Liz gave herself a shake. She was beginning to believe her own dreams.

"I was born and grew up in this house," Gran went on. "So were my mother and her mother before her. All of us named Elizabeth. Like you, Liz. And like your mom."

Liz nodded. She knew all that. She was Liz. Her mother was Beth. Gran was Betty. All of them were nicknames of Elizabeth. "So what were the Elizabeths before us called?" she asked.

Gran shrugged. "Just Elizabeth, I think. I know my mother was never called anything else." As she spoke, her gaze was caught by the house. She looked sad.

"Why are you selling the house, Gran?" Liz asked softly. She reached to take her grandmother's hand.

At first Liz thought Gran wasn't going to answer. She just went on looking and looking at the house. At last she said, "I love this old place. I always have. But it's too far to drive all the way up here from Minneapolis. Your mom worries about me when I stay here by myself. So . . ." She straightened her back and squeezed Liz's hand.

"So," she said again, "it's time. That's why I brought you with me . . . to help me pack away my past. And to be my guardian angel so your mom won't worry."

"I will be your guardian angel," Liz promised. She threw her arms around her grandmother and gave her a hard hug. "Always."

Gran hugged her back. "I wanted you to see the house, too," she said. "So you'll remember. I guess for me it's . . . it's . . ." Her voice trailed off.

Liz stepped back to study her grandmother's face. "What is it for you?" she asked. She really wanted to know.

Gran smiled down at Liz. "For me, dear Liz, this house is about connections. Connections with all the people who came before us. My grandmother used to tell me stories about them. It's like they are still here. Can you feel it, too?"

Liz thought about being called awake with the name "Elizabeth." She thought about the blue light and the woman who had passed through the wall next to her bed. And despite the warm sunlight, ice water trickled down her spine.

"Yes," she said to her grandmother. "I can feel it."

3
Again

Gran and Liz spent the morning washing the cupboards and sorting their contents. Most of the dishes and pots and pans would stay behind to be sold with the house. Gran chose a few things to take home with her. Liz found a salt and pepper shaker set shaped like a chicken and a rooster that Gran said she could have. She tucked them away in the pocket of her suitcase.

Gran had always been a hard worker. She did everything around her house in the city. Last summer she had even climbed up on her roof to fix some shingles. (Mom had been really mad about that.) But after lunch, she looked tired.

"It's been a long morning," she said to Liz. "I think I'll take a nap." And she went upstairs.

Liz cleaned for a while longer. But the work was no fun without Gran. She wandered into her bedroom and looked around. Was there something in the trunk the blue woman had wanted her to see? She tried the lid.

The trunk was locked. Liz didn't know where to look for a key.

Liz lay down on the narrow bed and put one hand against the wall. She chose the same spot where the blue woman had gone through. But nothing had changed. It was still as solid as . . . well, as solid as a wall.

She rolled onto her back and closed her eyes. She hated naps. Sleeping in the daytime just made her feel muzzy. When she woke, she usually felt worse than she had before she slept. But at least a nap would take up some time until Gran was ready to start working again.

What had Gran meant by her being a

guardian angel? Probably nothing, really.

Grown-ups were funny that way. They used words like *angel*, but they didn't really mean them.

Liz let herself sink a little deeper into the bed.

And that was when she heard it. Laughter. It sounded like kids this time. A bunch of little kids messing around.

The playing sounds grew louder. Calling, giggling. Someone was trying to quiet them. "Hush," a female voice said. "Hush! The baby is sleeping. You mustn't be so loud!"

The voices quieted, but not entirely. Liz

held her breath, straining to hear. Was it the woman she had seen last night? Was she the one hushing the children?

Then she heard it again. They were whispering now! And then more laughter. This time the other voice joined in the giggling. Whoever it was didn't sound like a grown-up woman.

Liz sat up slowly. She stared at the wall. She didn't have to touch it again to know it was still solid. But somehow the sound came from there.

She strained her ears. She half hoped to hear something more. But only half. The other half would be happy if what lay on the other side of the wall stayed a dream.

"Elizabeth! Come find me, Elizabeth!"

Liz gasped. There it was again! *Elizabeth!* But this time it wasn't the woman's voice.

She climbed off the bed. Tugging at the wooden frame, she pulled it away from the wall. When eight or ten inches had opened up, she walked around and stepped into the open space. She stood facing the wall.

"Elizabeth!" Liz heard once more. "Can you find me?"

Liz's heart pounded. Slowly she raised her hands. She pressed both palms against the wall's smooth surface. Then she closed her eyes.

"Elizabeth!"

Somehow she had to answer that call! Liz took a deep breath, then she stepped forward. Her nose crunched against the wall.

She stepped back, rubbing her nose. Her cheeks blazed. How could she be so silly?

There was no sound now, nothing at all. Maybe there had never been any sound. Maybe she was imagining the whole thing. Maybe . . .

But she didn't know any other maybes. And she didn't believe any of the ones she had thought of.

"Elizabeth!" The voice came again. It

was farther away this time. Faint and far away. "Elizabeth!"

Liz pressed both palms against the wall and stood perfectly still. She listened. She waited.

She wasn't Elizabeth. She was only Liz. Why, then, did she feel so certain that the voice was calling her?

And why did it feel as if she could pass through this very solid wall if she only tried?

4
A Visit

When Gran woke from her nap, she said, "We've done enough work for one day. Do you want to go fishing?"

Liz did.

They walked down to the lake and stood on the rickety old dock with their poles. They caught only sunnies, but Liz liked sunnies. Gran cleaned them and dipped them in egg and cornmeal. Then she fried them in her cast-iron pan until

they were crisp and golden brown.

Liz went to bed that night before dark had even settled around the old house. The late-June sun didn't set until after ten o'clock this far north, so Gran didn't seem especially surprised when Liz said she was ready. She wasn't tired, though. She was ready for something else. She was ready to listen for the voices.

She thought several times of telling Gran what was going on, but she didn't. She wasn't sure why.

Instead, she lay perfectly still, listening. Nothing happened. No whispers. No blue light. No laughing children.

The next thing Liz knew, light had crept into the room again. She rose on one elbow and gazed at the morning. Then slowly, carefully, she reached a hand to the wall next to her bed. Only an ordinary hard surface. And the sounds coming from the other side were ordinary, too. Gran was making breakfast. Liz heard the refrigerator door open and close. She smelled bacon frying.

She flopped back down onto the bed, pulled the covers to her chin, and closed her eyes.

Liz didn't know how long she had been lying there when she heard the crying. A baby? It sounded like a baby. There was no baby in Gran's house.

But then there were no giggling children, either.

She sat up slowly, holding her breath. She turned to face the wall. This time she didn't touch it. Instead, she just sat there, cross-legged on the bed, waiting.

Now she could hear someone talking. It was the kind of singsong talk people used to soothe babies.

Slowly the crying let up. Then . . . silence.

Was that all? Would there be nothing more?

The bed was still pushed away from the wall. Liz dropped her feet into the opening between the bed and the wall. She stood and closed her eyes. After a few breaths, she took a small step forward. Another. Then another.

Each time she took a step, she squeezed her eyes shut harder. She kept expecting to bump into the wall.

She didn't.

She took a few more steps and stopped. Her heart pounded. Slowly she opened her eyes and drew in a long, slow breath.

Liz no longer stood in the little bedroom with the trunk. Instead, she was in a log cabin. It was the log cabin her great-great-grandfather had built before the extra wall was added. She was certain of that.

She faced a window that was exactly like the one over Gran's kitchen sink. It had four panes of wavery glass. A low wooden

dresser stood below it now instead of a sink. A girl was changing a baby on the dresser top. She was probably only a year or two older than Liz.

Three little boys sat at a table eating something that looked like oatmeal from

wooden bowls. They gaped at Liz. Their spoons stopped in the air in front of their faces, and they stared and stared.

Liz stared back. They all looked solid enough. She didn't think they would suddenly disappear the way the woman had. But she couldn't be sure.

Liz turned back to the girl. She wore a faded cotton dress that reached to her ankles and no shoes. Her hair fell over her shoulders in two chestnut-brown braids. Liz touched her own hair. It was almost the same color, but not nearly as long.

Liz neither moved nor spoke. She wasn't entirely sure she could.

Finally, the largest of the little boys cried, "Elizabeth! Look! There be somebody here. Behind you."

The girl—was she Elizabeth?—whirled. She gasped when she saw Liz. She snatched up the baby and clutched him so hard that he let out a small cry. Her eyes were a vivid blue. Her face had gone as pale as paste.

Liz put out a hand to calm the girl. "I'm Liz," she said. "I've come . . ." But she stopped. She had no idea why she had come or how she had gotten here.

"Oh!" the girl cried. "Oh . . . oh . . . oh!" And then, to Liz's surprise, she fell on her knees. She let the baby slide gently to the floor. "My guardian angel!" she said.

Guardian angel! Liz took a step backward. This girl really meant it!

Elizabeth reached her hands up as if in prayer. "Mama always told me I had a guardian angel. And here you be!"

Liz was too shocked to speak. And since she couldn't think of anything else to do, she took another step backward.

The baby was clearly outraged to find himself on the floor. He screwed up his face for a long, silent moment. Then he opened his mouth and began to howl.

Liz took two more steps away from the girl and the baby's noise. Something cool against the back of her legs stopped her. She didn't even check to make sure it was her bed. She just collapsed onto it.

And when she looked up again, the girl, the baby, the little boys at the table . . . all had disappeared. Even the baby's cry had faded away.

Nothing remained but the wall.

5
Guardian Angel!

Liz sat on the bed, unable to move.

Guardian angel! That girl thought she, Liz, was a guardian angel! A real one! She covered her mouth with one hand to hold back a laugh.

But then she looked down at her long pink nightgown. Gran had made it for her and it did look like the dresses angels wore in pictures. And Liz had to admit that she had shown up in the room rather suddenly.

A visit from an angel probably made as much sense as a girl stepping through a wall from the twenty-first century.

This time Liz did laugh. Right out loud. Then she stopped herself. She didn't want Gran sticking her head in the door to ask what was funny. What would she tell her? *Did you know that I'm a guardian angel? Just like you said?*

Liz giggled quietly.

Anyway, she rather liked being taken for an angel. The idea made the other strange things seem almost normal. Like walking through a wall into another time. Or a woman appearing in a blue light.

Who were these people, anyway? The girl and all the little boys? The woman? Maybe the girl was her great-great . . . But Liz didn't know how many *greats* to put before the word *grandmother.* At least she knew her name was Elizabeth.

So that's who the voice had been calling just now! Maybe the blue woman had been calling that Elizabeth, too!

Liz's head was filled with questions. She reached for her clothes. She could at least find out who that girl might be. She wanted to know, too, why the woman she saw was so different from the rest. The girl and the children had looked solid. They had seemed as real as Liz herself. But the woman was more like a ghost. If you wanted to believe in ghosts!

Liz dressed quickly and went to the kitchen. Gran was mixing up pancakes. Bacon sizzled on the stove.

"Good morning, Gran," she said. "Smells good." She settled at the wooden table. After a moment, she said, "I've been wondering. Who built this log cabin? I mean, how many *greats* ago was he?"

"He was my great-grandfather. So let's see . . . he was your great-great-great-grandfather." Gran counted the *greats* off on her fingers.

"And his kids? There must have been kids."

Gran smiled. "If there had been no children, you and your mother and I wouldn't be here. There were four, I think. No . . . five of them."

"One girl and four boys," Liz supplied. "The boys were all younger than the girl."

Gran turned to give Liz a puzzled stare. "How did you know that?" she asked.

"I . . . I . . ." Liz felt caught. Should she tell Gran how she knew? Gran would never laugh at her. She knew that. Still, the girl, Elizabeth, felt like her secret now. "I guess Mom must have told me," she lied. And she shrugged as though none of it was very important, after all.

Gran nodded. She turned back to her pancakes. "The girl," she went on, "was the first Elizabeth. She was your great-great-grandmother."

"And her mother? She must have had a mother."

"She died soon after the last baby was born. Elizabeth wouldn't have been much older than you at the time. But she was the one who raised all those boys."

Liz thought about what she had seen, the three little boys at the table and the crying baby. How could a girl not much older than she was manage to take care of all those children?

And if the woman in the blue light was Elizabeth's mother, then she really *was* a ghost!

Liz shivered at the thought.

"But what about their father?" she demanded. "Didn't he help?"

"As best he could, I imagine," Gran replied. "But he was a farmer. Farming was backbreaking work then. Dawn-to-dusk backbreaking work. He probably didn't have much time for the children. Elizabeth must have done most of the caretaking."

Liz considered. What more did she need

to know? *Gran, did you ever step through the wall in the bedroom? Have you ever been in the old log cabin yourself?* But she couldn't ask that.

"Do you believe in guardian angels?" she asked instead. "I mean . . . really?"

Gran poured a pancake into the hot pan. When she turned to Liz, her eyebrows were raised. Clearly it wasn't a question she had expected. She answered simply, though. "My mother used to tell us we each had our own guardian angel."

"Did you believe her?"

Gran was silent for a moment, thinking. "Yes. I'm sure I did. I guess I half believe her even now. Mostly, though, I think we're meant to be guardian angels for one another. Don't you?"

Liz took a slow, deep breath. She quite liked that idea. "What are we going to do today?" she asked.

"I thought we'd go swimming first," Gran told her. "Then I want to go through that big trunk in your room."

The trunk! Was that what the blue woman had been trying to tell her to do . . . to open the trunk?

"I wonder what we'll find," Liz said. She said it casually, but her heart pounded.

6
The Croup

The whole time Liz swam, she kept thinking about the trunk. Something important must be in there!

But when she and Gran returned to the house, Gran couldn't find the right key. She found several keys in a dresser drawer in the small bedroom. None of them fit.

Gran laid a hand on the curved lid. "It's strange. I don't remember ever looking inside. Still . . . I keep thinking that whatever is in here must be important."

Reluctantly, they decided to sort out the closets instead. One was filled with games like Monopoly and Scrabble. Some of those they packed up to go to Gran's house in the city. Others they put back on the shelves.

"Whoever buys this place will enjoy them on rainy days," Gran said.

With every box they packed, Gran seemed to grow quieter.

"I wish you didn't have to sell the house," Liz said at last.

Gran smiled, but the smile seemed sad. "It's time," she said. "Your parents have their own lake cabin. Who would use this old place?"

Liz had to admit she liked her parents' cabin best. Still, she wished she could take away Gran's sadness. The best she could think of was to make them both chocolate-ripple ice cream cones. Their favorite. She heaped the ice cream high, and they sat on the back steps and licked and licked.

A chipmunk with lumpy cheeks ran in and out from under the house. He was carrying seeds to store. "I hope the new people like chipmunks," Liz said.

"And raccoons," Gran added. "Not to mention a bear or two. The ones who are too fierce to be scared off by raccoons."

They both laughed.

And ghosts, Liz thought. But she didn't say that.

That night after Liz went to bed, it happened again. There she was . . . suddenly awake and sitting up in the middle of the bed, not knowing what had awakened her.

When Liz heard the strange noise, the skin on her arms pricked into goose bumps.

The sound was hard to describe and impossible to identify. A breathy screech? A whistle being sucked on instead of blown? She had never heard anything quite like it before.

Something about it said *trouble,* though. Serious trouble. Liz leapt out of bed. Her toe hit the wall. She doubled over, grabbing her foot to squeeze away the pain.

"Elizabeth," whispered a voice. "Elizabeth!"

When Liz straightened, the blue woman stood before her. She seemed to be halfway through the wall. She lifted a hand for Liz to follow.

Without even considering that she had any other choice, Liz did.

She hadn't taken more than three steps,

though, before the blue woman vanished. Without her light, the darkness was total. Liz couldn't even see the bed she had left behind. The breathy, whistling sound, however, grew louder, closer. In addition to the whistle, now she heard a murmuring voice.

"Elizabeth?" Liz called. "Is that you?"

"Who are you?" came the reply from the darkness. The voice trembled slightly.

"I'm Liz," Liz replied. And it seemed easiest to say, "I think I'm your guardian angel."

"My guardian angel?" There was a clanking sound—the stove door opening?—and a candle flickered. "But you said, 'I think.'

Wouldn't a guardian angel know? I mean . . . whether you be my angel or no." The face lit by the candle looked worried.

"I am," Liz told her. She made her voice sound certain. After all, hadn't Gran said we are all meant to be one another's guardian angels? "Your guardian angel, I mean. I'm sure of it."

Elizabeth set the candle into a holder on the table. She stood next to the table, the baby in her arms. The strange noise came from him. Each time he drew in his breath, that whistling sound came again. Every breath took such an effort that Liz thought he would quit trying. But he couldn't do that, of course. The moment he did, he would die!

"What's wrong?" Liz asked, moving toward them. "Why is he breathing like that?"

"He has the croup," Elizabeth told her.

Liz wasn't sure what "the croup" was. Clearly, though, it was dangerous. "And your father?" she asked. "Where is he?" He couldn't still be farming in the middle of the night.

"He's gone to fetch the doctor." Elizabeth lifted the gasping baby high above her head as though the air might be better up there.

"Oh . . . the doctor!" Liz relaxed a little. Then everything would be all right.

"Only . . ." Elizabeth lowered the baby and kissed his forehead. Her mouth trembled. She was struggling to hold back tears.

"Only what?" Liz asked gently.

The answer came in a rush. "Only the doctor be hours away. So Pa will not return until near on to noon. I am afeard poor Matthew cannot last so long."

And then, to Liz's surprise, Elizabeth thrust the wheezing baby into her arms and added, "I am so glad you have come! We do need an angel here."

A chill raced across Liz's skin. She had let Elizabeth think she really was her guardian angel. And now the girl was counting on her to help! And what did she know about sick babies? Nothing.

What help could she bring? Absolutely none.

7
"Booke of Remedys"

The baby in Liz's arms began to cry. His voice was deep and hoarse. When the crying stopped, it was only to be replaced by a brassy cough. He had a fever, too. He might have been a tiny stove the way heat poured off of him.

If only she could talk to Gran. Gran knew about sick babies.

But if she gave Matthew to Elizabeth and went back to her own time, she might not be able to get here again. She hadn't had very good luck returning when she had tried before. And the baby's lips were turning blue!

Matthew sat heavily in Liz's arms. He coughed and wheezed and sobbed. Liz hugged him to her and looked around the small cabin. She had to find something that would help. There were bunks at one side where the other boys were sleeping. A table sat at the other side, a cast-iron stove in the middle. And . . . Liz gasped.

Here was the woman again, the woman made of blue light.

"Look!" Liz cried, pointing.

Elizabeth turned to look, but her face remained blank.

"Don't you see?" Liz asked.

Elizabeth looked at Liz again. She shook her head. Clearly she saw nothing. "Please," she begged. "You must help our Matthew. Whether you be an angel or no, you must. I fear we have little hope except for you."

Little hope except for me? Liz wanted to drop the baby and run. Instead, she turned back to the woman on the other side of the room. The blue figure hovered over a wooden trunk with a rounded lid. It was the same as the trunk in Liz's bedroom!

"That trunk!" Liz pointed. "Tell me what's in it."

Elizabeth stared at the trunk, then at Liz. "My mama's belongings," she said. "But—"

"Let's open it," Liz replied. "I think there is something in there that will help!" She handed the baby back to Elizabeth and hurried to the trunk. But, as before, the brass hasp was locked.

"Where's the key?" she cried.

Elizabeth took a large key down from a nail set in the wood frame of the window. The nail and the key were hidden by burlap curtains. "Here it is," she said. "But I do not know what you will find to help in there. It is just Mama's dresses and such."

Liz took the key. She had to find something in the trunk. Otherwise there was no hope. Certainly *she* didn't know anything about babies with the croup.

Her hands trembled as she fitted the key to the lock. She turned it until it clicked. Then she lifted the lid and began to sort quickly through the contents. She didn't know what she was looking for. She knew only that this was where Elizabeth's mother wanted her to look. Under a silk dress were sheets, a pair of silver candlesticks, a Bible, a black lace shawl. And when she gently lifted the shawl, she found a small handwritten booklet.

"What's this?" she asked. She held it up for Elizabeth to see.

"I think it be my mother's book of remedies," she said. "I had quite forgotten it."

"Remedies? Like for making people well?"

"People and cattle and all manner of creatures," Elizabeth replied. "Mama knew much of medicine. People came from far—"

"That's it!" Liz broke in. "Don't you see? The book will tell you what to do about the baby's croup!"

For an instant, Elizabeth's face glowed. But when Liz thrust the small hand-lettered book toward her, she didn't lift a hand to take it. She just stood there, shaking her head.

"What's the matter?" Liz pleaded. "Your mother wanted you to have this. I know she did."

Elizabeth only lowered her head. In a small voice that Liz strained to hear over the baby's wheezing, she said, "I cannot read."

Liz was amazed. "Why not?" she asked. "Everyone knows how to read!"

Elizabeth's head came up. "We have had no school here. We will not have school until a master comes next winter. Mama was going to teach me, but there be so many babies. She never had time. And Pa does not know himself."

"Ah," Liz said. Only that. So that was why she was here. Maybe she was, indeed, Elizabeth's angel. An angel who could read.

Liz flipped through the small book. When she came upon "The Croup," she read the page eagerly.

"Quick! A wet cloth," she told Elizabeth. "A wet cloth to put over his face. And build up the fire in the stove. We have to boil water and make a tent to fill with steam!"

The two girls started the tasks. The

baby seemed to sense that help was at hand. He watched everything they did with enormous eyes. The blue woman hovered in the corner of the room as the girls worked. Strangely, Liz found the ghost comforting.

At last, they settled beneath a blanket tent with baby Matthew. When the kettle began boiling, the steam quickly filled the tent. Matthew rested his cheek against Elizabeth's shoulder. After a time, his breathing grew quieter.

They sat side by side under the blanket tent. The candle glowed at their feet. Liz tried to think of something to say.

"It will be good when you can go to school," she said at last.

"I do not expect to go," Elizabeth told her. "A big girl like me who has not learned to read—"

"Could learn very quickly," Liz broke in.

Elizabeth's chin came up sharply. She stared at Liz in disbelief. Then slowly a smile began to bloom across her face. "Do you think?" she asked.

"You could," Liz told her. "You must believe me. I'm your angel."

Elizabeth nodded. "I could learn," she repeated. "Surely."

Matthew's eyelids fluttered toward sleep.

"Be you truly an angel?" Elizabeth asked after another silence. She looked deeply into Liz's eyes.

Liz smiled at her. "Whoever I am," she answered, "your mother sent me."

8
A Story

Liz woke in her own bed. Or rather, she woke in her bed in Gran's old house. The morning was cool, but strands of hair clung damply to her face. She remembered steaming beneath the blanket and smiled.

She didn't know when or how she had returned to her own time, but she was glad to be back.

Gran poked her head into the room. "You're a sleepyhead today," she said.

"Sorry," Liz replied. She sat up, and Gran came to sit on the side of her bed.

"Tell me more about Elizabeth, would you?" Liz asked. "The first Elizabeth, I mean. What did she do when she grew up?"

"The first Elizabeth?" Gran folded her hands in her lap. "Why . . . let me think. She became a doctor. She married and had four children, too."

"She became a *what*?"

Gran smiled. "Yes. It was unusual for that time, but she became a doctor. The man she married owned the stable in the small town where she lived. He used to drive the carriage when she went to see her patients. I guess that's when they fell in love."

Liz leaned back against the headboard of the bed. So Elizabeth had gone to school. And she had learned more than reading, too. Could it be that Liz had made a difference in Elizabeth's life? It didn't seem possible. Still . . . she couldn't help wondering.

"What about her brother Matthew? The baby. Did he grow up all right?"

"Matthew? Oh . . . he became—" Gran stopped. She stared at Liz. "How did you know Matthew's name?"

Liz laughed. "You must have told me.

When we were talking about the little boys yesterday. You must have said his name then. Didn't you?"

Gran shrugged. "Well, anyway, he became a college professor. He taught mathematics."

Liz tried to imagine that round-faced baby standing in front of a class droning on about math. She couldn't, but the idea made her laugh again.

"Oh . . ." She stopped suddenly and jumped off the bed. "I just remembered."

"What is it?" Gran asked.

But Liz was already looking behind the curtain. And there it was, the nail in the window frame with the brass key hanging on it.

"Here," she said. She turned and held it up for Gran to see. "It's the key for the trunk."

"How did you know to look there?" Gran asked. She took the key and fit it into the trunk's lock. When the trunk was open, she bent eagerly over it. She seemed to have forgotten her own question.

Liz peered into the open trunk, too.

The contents had changed since she had looked in it on the other side of the wall. She could see that at a glance. The trunk was filled with yellowed sheets, a torn quilt, some limp towels. Gran took them all out and piled them on the floor.

"They're pretty ragged," she said. "I don't think there is anything here worth saving."

And then, to Liz's surprise, Gran burst into tears.

"Oh, Gran," Liz cried. She threw her arms around her grandmother's neck. "What's wrong? Tell me. Please!"

Gran hugged Liz. Then she sat back, wiping her tears with the backs of her hands. "It's nothing . . . really," she sniffed. "I guess I'd been sure I had something special in the trunk. Photos, maybe. Something to remind me of the old house when I can't see it anymore."

"Well," Liz said. She picked up the moth-eaten quilt. "You could put this on your bed."

They both laughed.

"Anyway," Gran said, "tears are probably the best cure for a touch of sadness. Or the second best, anyway."

"What's the best?" Liz asked.

"Don't you know?"

Liz shook her head. She didn't know. She didn't have any idea.

Gran took a tissue out of her pocket and blew her nose. "Then I'll tell you," she said. "It's sharing your bit of sadness with another Elizabeth."

Liz felt warm all over. She lifted the last blanket from the trunk and looked beneath it. And that was when she saw it!

A handwritten booklet lay on the very bottom of the trunk. On the front it said, "Booke of Remedys."

"Oh, Gran. Look!" Liz cried. She picked it up and handed it to her grandmother.

Gran stared at the booklet. "I wonder who this belonged to. I can't remember ever seeing it before." Her voice was filled with wonder.

"Open it," Liz begged. "Read what it says about croup."

Gran looked at her strangely, but she leafed through the booklet until she found the place. "The Croup," she read. "A wet cloth over the face sometimes helps. But the best remedy is to boil a kettle or pots of water. Make a tent over the boiling pots so the sufferer can breathe in the steam."

Liz nodded. "It works," she said.

Gran studied the page closely. Then she studied Liz. "When I was a girl," she began

at last. She paused, then started again. "When I was a girl, sometimes I used to think I heard voices in this room. Voices calling 'Elizabeth.' Once I even thought I saw a—" She stopped, as though the word were too hard to say.

"A ghost?" Liz supplied.

Gran nodded. "How did you know? I never told anyone."

Liz took her grandmother's hand. "You tell me about your ghost," she said. "And I'll tell you about mine."

Her grandmother wiped away the last of the tears. Then she smiled and leaned back against the trunk. "A good story might be the very best cure of all," she said. "Why don't you start?"

And so Liz did. "It all began," she said, "with a blue ghost."

About the Author

Marion Dane Bauer is the author of more than forty books for children, including the Newbery Honor Book *On My Honor* and *Rain of Fire,* which won a Jane Addams Children's Book Award. She has also won the Kerlan Award for her collected work. Marion teaches writing and is on the faculty of the Vermont College Master of Fine Arts in Writing for Children and Young Adults program.

Marion has two grown children and five grandchildren and lives with her partner, Ann Goddard, in Eden Prairie, Minnesota.